This edition published in 1990 by Gallery Books,
an imprint of W.H. Smith Publishers, Inc.
112 Madison Avenue, New York, New York 10016

Produced for Gallery Books by Joshua Morris Publishing, Inc.,
221 Danbury Road, Wilton, CT 06897

Copyright © 1990 Joshua Morris Publishing, Inc.
All rights reserved. Printed in Hong Kong.
ISBN 0-8317-7258-1

Gallery Books are available for bulk purchase
for sales promotions and premium use.
For details write or telephone the Manager of Special Sales,
W.H. Smith Publishers, Inc., 112 Madison Avenue,
New York, New York 10016   (212) 532-6600.

The Ugly Duckling

Retold by Jane Resnick
Illustrated by Yuri Saltzman

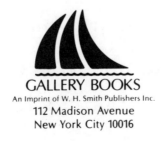

GALLERY BOOKS
An Imprint of W. H. Smith Publishers Inc.
112 Madison Avenue
New York City 10016

It was summer on the farm.

"Peep, peep, peep!" cried three pretty, yellow ducklings as they tumbled out of their shells.

But there was still one egg left in the nest.

Finally, the last egg began to crack.

"Tweep," said the fourth duckling when he climbed out of the nest.

But he wasn't pretty like the other ducklings. He was big and ugly, and his feathers were gray.

The next morning, the mother duck led her little family to the pond. She jumped into the water calling, "Come on, children."

Splash! One by one the ducklings followed her into the pond and swam behind her.

The other ducks on the farm all admired the three pretty ducklings, but they laughed at the poor ugly duckling.

"He's so ugly!" they said.

"Looks aren't important," quacked the mother duck. "Besides, he's a very good swimmer."

Time passed. Every day the animals on the farm teased the ugly duckling. When the cows and sheep came to the pond for a drink, they made the duckling feel terrible.

"Go away," mooed the cows.

"You're ugly," baad the sheep.

One afternoon, the other ducks laughed so hard at the ugly duckling's skinny, long neck that he ran away from the farm!

"I'm never going back there," said the little duckling.

Some days later, the tired duckling came to a small cottage where a cat and a hen lived. The cat could arch his back and make sparks if his fur was rubbed the wrong way. And the hen could lay more eggs than you could count.

The duckling knocked at the door. When the cat and the hen opened it, he asked if he could stay with them.

"Can you do something useful like making sparks or laying eggs?" they asked.

"No," said the duckling.

"Then you can't stay here," they said and closed the door.

By fall, the duckling was living on a lonely pond in the middle of the forest. His only company day after day was his own sad reflection in the water. He was very unhappy.

Then one chilly evening, the duckling saw a
flock of snow-white swans flying over head.
"Such beautiful birds!" he thought. But soon
they were gone, and he was sadder than ever.

Winter came to the pond. One cold night, the poor duckling almost froze. Luckily a farmer came by the pond. When he saw the duckling, he wrapped him up tenderly in his coat and took him home.

At the farmer's house, the farmer's children laughed at the ugly duckling. He was so frightened that he flew up to the table, tipped over a pitcher of milk, knocked down a bag of flour, and fell KERPLOP! into the butter tub. What a mess he was. Dripping milk, flour, and butter, the duckling ran out the door.

Back at the pond again, the duckling spent a
lonely winter. When spring finally came, the lovely
white swans came back to the pond.

"If I go over to them, they will tell me to go
away," he thought. "But I'm so lonely that I am
going to try to make friends anyway."

The ugly duckling swam to the swans saying, "I know I'm ugly, but please be my friends." And he hung his head down sadly.

But all winter the duckling had been growing and changing. So when he looked down at his reflection, he was amazed. He wasn't an ugly duckling anymore. He was a beautiful SWAN!

"Look!" cried a child playing on the bank of the pond. "There's another swan, and he's the prettiest swan of all."

The new swan lifted his wings to show his beautiful feathers. He was happy at last.